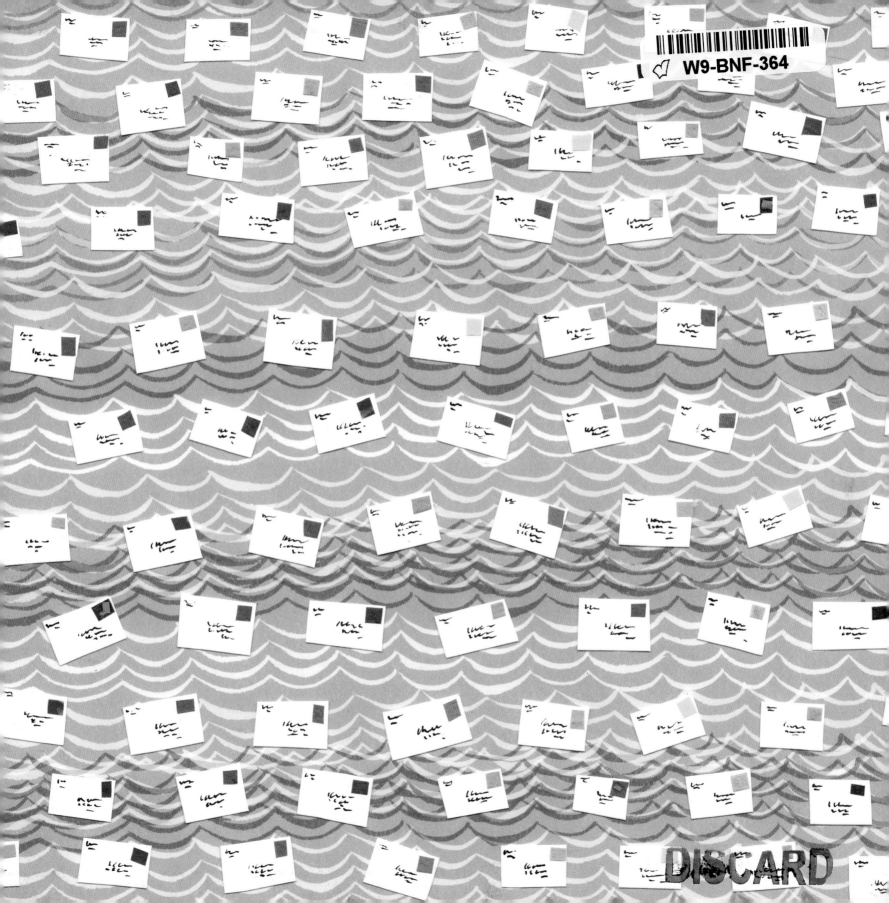

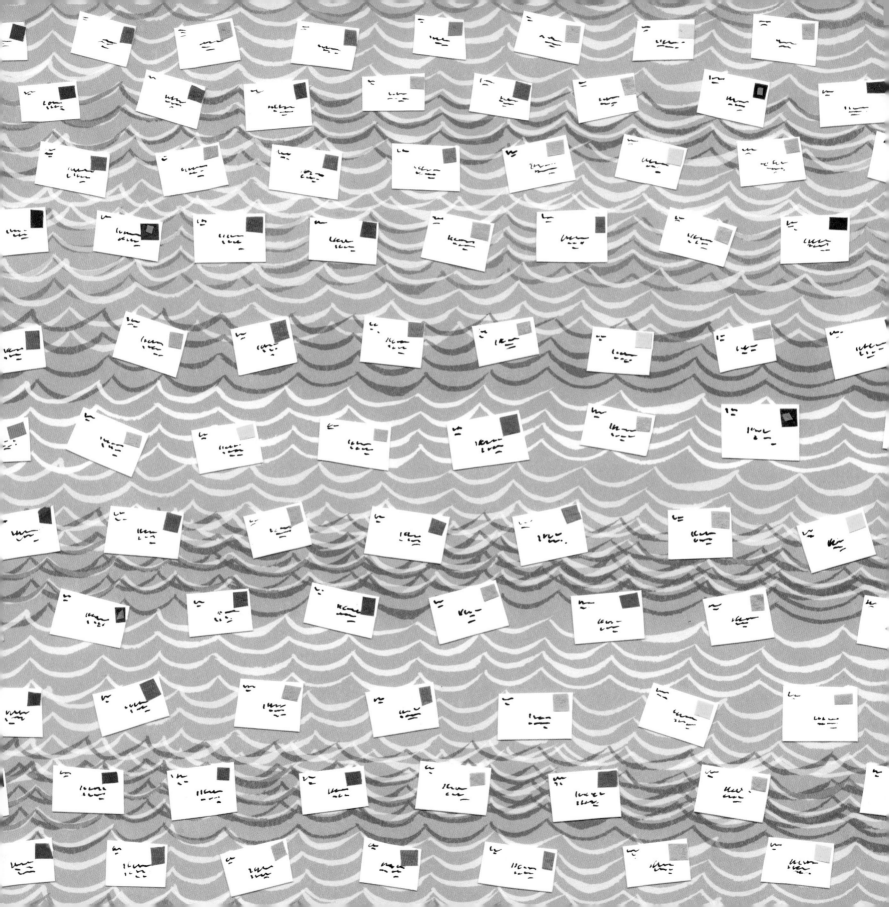

every color

erin eitter kono

 dial books for young readers

For Caitlyn Akiko, my adventurer

The friends' journey includes the following countries and landmarks: the Netherlands (windmill);
England (London Bridge, St. Paul's Cathedral, and Big Ben); France (Notre Dame, Eiffel Tower, and Louvre
Museum); Italy (Rialto Bridge and Piazza San Marco); Greece (Parthenon and Santorini); Turkey (Hagia Sophia,
the Blue Mosque, and Cappadocia); Egypt (Great Sphinx and pyramid); India (Taj Mahal); China (Great Wall);
Japan (Matsumoto Castle); Australia (Sydney Opera House and Great Barrier Reef); Chile (Easter Island);
Brazil (Christ the Redeemer statue); and United States of America (Statue of Liberty).

Dial Books for Young Readers
Penguin Young Readers Group
An imprint of Penguin Random House LLC
375 Hudson Street
New York, NY 10014

Design by Lily Malcom • Text set in Blockhead • The art was created using mixed media on Moab Entrada paper.

Bear lived at the top of the world.
He was surrounded by white ice
and white snow,
and he longed for color.

His friends tried their best to cheer him,
but it was no use.

Then a passing seagull had an idea.

The seagull knew a girl with just the right gift to share.

It was the most amazing thing Bear had ever received.

But the gift didn't take away his discontent.

When Bear's thank you note arrived—
Seagull Express—the girl realized
that she needed to go to him. She
understood that he looked for
color, but could not see it.

She rigged her skiff and sailed across the ocean.

"Come with me," said the girl when she finally reached Bear.
"I know where to find what you need."

Bear bid farewell to his friends, and off he and the girl sailed.

They traveled beyond distant shores,

up rivers

and down,

through golden cities

and hills of green,

exploring wonder

after wonder

after wonder

until they'd seen all that they could.

Then the girl trimmed her sails
and returned Bear to the icy north.

There, proudly displayed by his friends,
were all the paintings from Bear's journey.
He gasped.
His white home reflected every color of the rainbow.

It always had.

He'd just needed to learn how to see them.

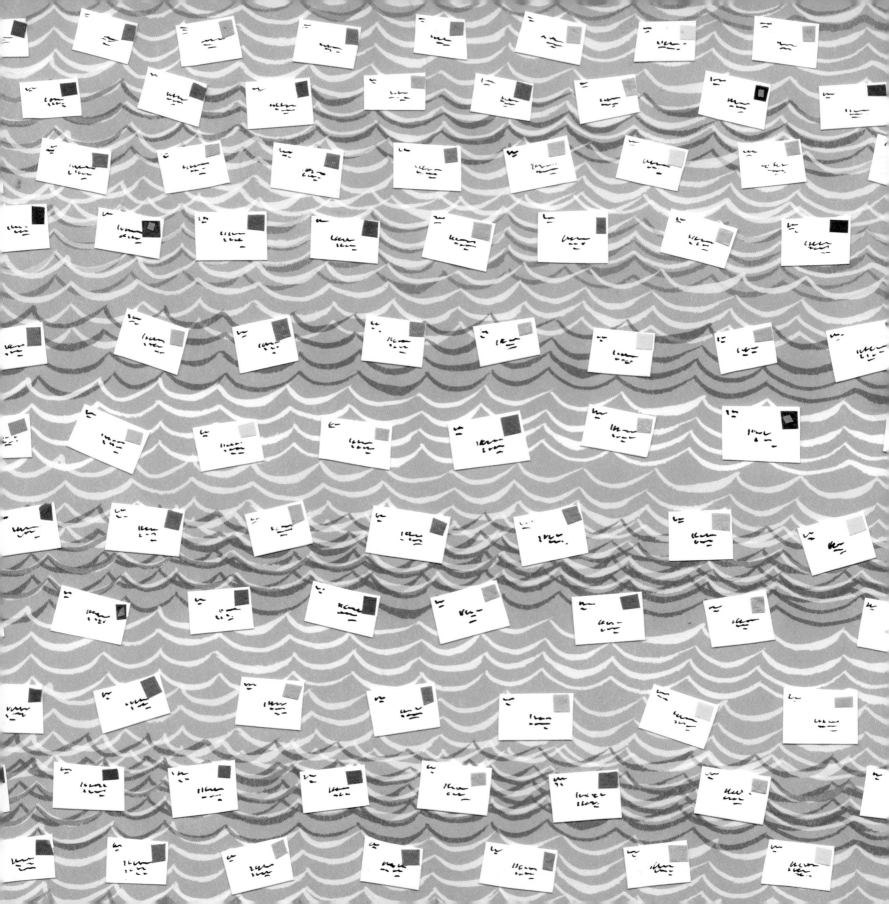